There are some players born to play ball.
—Joe DiMaggio

And there are some players who are not.
—Sarah

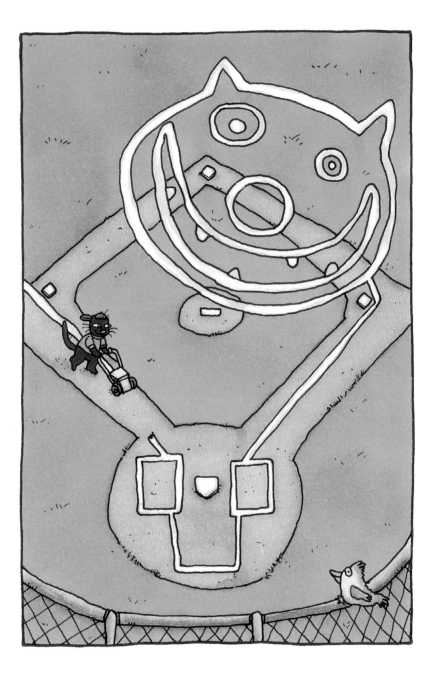

Three Strikes for
ROTTEN
RALPH

Written by Jack Gantos

Illustrated by Nicole Rubel

Farrar Straus Giroux

New York

For Mabel   —J.G.

For my family   —N.R.

Text copyright © 2011 by Jack Gantos
Pictures copyright © 2011 by Nicole Rubel
All rights reserved
Distributed in Canada by D&M Publishers, Inc.
Color separations by Chroma Graphics
Printed in October 2010 in China by South China Printing Co. Ltd.,
Dongguan City, Guangdong Province
Designed by Natalie Zanecchia
First edition, 2011
1 3 5 7 9 10 8 6 4 2

www.fsgkidsbooks.com

Library of Congress Cataloging-in-Publication Data
Gantos, Jack.
    Three strikes for Rotten Ralph / written by Jack Gantos ; illustrated by
Nicole Rubel.— 1st ed.
        p. cm.
    Summary: When Rotten Ralph, the cat, fails to win a spot on a baseball
team with his friend Sarah, he becomes the "cat boy" instead, still dreaming
of proving himself the superstar he imagines himself to be.
    ISBN: 978-0-374-36354-3
    [1. Baseball—Fiction. 2. Cats—Fiction. 3. Teamwork (Sports)—Fiction.]
I. Rubel, Nicole, ill. II. Title.

PZ7.G15334Thr 2011
[E]—dc22
                                                        2009046091

The character of Rotten Ralph was originally created by
Jack Gantos and Nicole Rubel.

Contents

Tryouts • 7

Play Ball! • 19

A Superstar Is Born • 29

Swing for Glory • 37

Tryouts

Ralph and Sarah were waiting their turns to try out for the new Fighting Squirrels baseball team.

"I hope they pick me," said Sarah. She had been practicing for weeks. "It's my dream to be part of the team."

Ralph was dreaming, too. He imagined himself stepping up to the plate as the crowd cheered. He pictured himself hitting a winning home run. As he rounded the bases, his teammates shouted, "Superstar Ralph! Superstar Ralph!"

Just then, Sarah threw the ball. Ralph was still dreaming when it thumped him on the head.

"Ralph," cautioned Sarah, "you have to pay attention. When you play in a real game, you can never take your eye off the ball."

Sarah gave Ralph more tips. "When you step up to bat, kick some dirt at the plate," she instructed. "Stare the pitcher in the eye. Then put the fat part of the bat on the ball. Hit 'em where they ain't! And always remember, the game ain't over till it's over. So no celebrating until you win."

That was a lot for Ralph to remember. He just wanted to be a superstar, so he forgot everything Sarah taught him.

When it was Ralph's turn to try out
for the team, the coach hit him an easy
grounder. Ralph muffed it. And when
Ralph went to bat, he whiffed.

"Show me your speed," said the coach.

Ralph took off so fast he tripped and landed in the water bucket.

The coach was not impressed.

Next it was Sarah's turn, and she showed the coach she could do it all.

After tryouts the coach announced who made the team. Sarah did. But Ralph did not.

Ralph benched himself in the dugout. He hung his head. Everyone is better than me, he thought. He felt like a super-dud.

"We still need a bat boy," the coach announced.

"How about a cat boy?" Sarah quickly asked.

The coach liked the idea.

Yes! thought Ralph. I'll be the cat boy
while I wait for my big chance to show
everyone I'm a superstar!

17

Play Ball!

"Oh, Ralph," said Sarah, "you look so handsome in your uniform. Being the cat boy is a very important job, and the team really needs you to help us play our best."

That day Ralph was ready to show the coach he could be super helpful.

When the players showed up with new gloves, Ralph spit in them to make the leather soft.

"Ugh, cat spit!" cried a teammate.

"From now on, Ralph," Sarah advised, "I think it would be best if the players spit in their own gloves."

At the next game, Ralph gave catnip-flavored gum to the players.

After that, he argued a call with the umpire and kicked dirt on his shoes.

"Ralph," said the coach, "this is not helping the team. Maybe you should just do some regular bat boy jobs."

Whatever, thought Ralph.

So he stacked the bats and helmets. He smoothed out the base paths on the field. He swept the dugout. He washed socks. He picked the chewed gum off the bench.

At the next game the team mascot couldn't make it. Ralph had to wear the Mighty Fighting Squirrel costume.

"Look," said a kid from the other team. "It's a giant squirrel!"

They chased him around the ball field and up a tree.

How can I ever be a superstar, thought Ralph, when I'm dressed like a big super-nut?

A Superstar Is Born

"Ralph," said Sarah, "if you spent more time practicing instead of dreaming, you'd be a better player."

Sure, Ralph thought as he yawned.

"Put your best paw forward and that way you might get into a game."

Okay, he thought.

Ralph got a pen and practiced his fancy autograph.

Then he decorated his uniform to look like a winner.

He practiced being interviewed on TV. He imagined what he would say. "There is no *we* in *team*," he'd announce, "just *me*!"

"Ralph," said Sarah, "you need to get real and fit in with the team. We have a big game coming up, and you had better be ready if the coach needs you."

Ralph gave Sarah his special superstar smile. I'm ready, he thought to himself, and handed her his new Superstar Ralph baseball card.

Swing for Glory

During the big game, disaster struck. One of Sarah's teammates got sick. She had eaten a bad hot dog between innings. By the last inning, she had turned green.

The game was tied. Coach looked around. He had only one extra player on the bench. "Cat boy," he barked. "You're up. The team needs you now!"

"Oh, Ralph," said Sarah. "This is the big chance you have been dreaming about."

Ralph grabbed a bat and strolled to the plate. He waved to all his fans. He pointed the end of the bat toward home run territory.

The pitcher wound up and threw a rocket. Ralph took a mighty swing and missed.

The pitcher threw another. Ralph missed that one, too.

Suddenly, he wasn't feeling like a superstar.

"Remember," hollered Sarah. "Look the pitcher in the eye. And put the fat part of the bat on the ball!"

The pitcher threw the ball. Ralph
closed his eyes and took a lucky swing.
Whack!

The ball flew through the air, missed
the outfielder's glove, and rolled all the
way to the fence.

Ralph forgot what to do next.

"Run!" yelled the team.

He ran down the line as fast as he could.

"I'm a superstar!" he shouted. "I'm a superstar! I *really am* a superstar!"

As he rounded the bases, he began
to do his special superstar celebration
dance. But just before home plate, he
tripped over his tail and belly flopped
onto the catcher.

"You're out!" cried the ump.

His teammates groaned. Ralph crawled back to the dugout and sat by himself on the end of the bench. He had let everyone down.

Now it was Sarah's turn. The score
was still tied and the team was down to
their last out. She stood in the batter's
box. She dug in her heels. She looked
out at the pitcher. When the pitch came,
she smacked it over the fence.

"Home run!" shouted the coach. "We win!"

Sarah's teammates and Ralph cheered. As she crossed home plate, everyone piled on. Ralph piled on top of everyone.

Sarah was the hero of the game.

On the way home, Ralph was so proud of Sarah. "You are my superstar," Ralph purred.

"Oh, no," replied Sarah. "I'm a team player. But don't worry, Ralph. You will always be number one on my team."